Bee Bopp ™

Written by Stephen Cosgrove
Illustrated by Charles Reasoner

PRICE STERN SLOAN
Los Angeles

ISBN: 0-8431-2286-2

As you lay on a crisp fall day
In a warm and sunny place,
Don't look up into the skies;
Instead, look down
        And squint your eyes.
Squint your eyes so very tight,
And if you wish
        With all your might,
You'll find the land of
        Morethansmall.
For in this land live buggs,
        that's all.

A leaf fell from a tree in Buggville. Swept by the winds, it floated down the cobblestone streets. It swirled and twirled around a streetlamp, then lazily continued on its way. It dropped for a moment on the shoulder of Ezekial T. Bugg, the local parson, and then, with a mind of its own, it leaped high into the air and landed like a butterfly on the lawn of an empty bugg house.

A large truck rolled up to the house. It carried a sign that said, *"Buggville Moving and STORAGE."* The truck was followed by a bright red car with a funny horn that played a funny song.

Out of the car burst the most outrageous family you have ever seen. There was Farley T. Mouth, the fastest talking salesbugg this side of the Buggville River. He was dressed in a checkered suit and a purple tie. Behind him was his wife, Melba Z. Last and least was their daughter, Bee Bopp, who chewed gum and couldn't say a sentence without saying "Gee whiz!"

The day after they moved in, Bee Bopp enrolled at Buttonwood School. She hadn't been there but a moment or two when she started chewing gum and making smart remarks. "Gee whiz, this school shouldn't be called Buttonwood it should be called Muttonhead where all the gluttonheads go to school!" Then she just laughed and laughed, thinking she was very funny.

The school secretary, Mizz Prizz, just glared over her glasses and filled out the forms.

Bee Bopp finished with the forms just in time to join the other buggs at recess. She went out to the playground and looked around. "Gee whiz," she shouted at the top of her lungs, "this place is dumb!" Just then she was jostled by a glasses-wearing bugg whose name was Glance.

"Whoops! Excuse me!" he said as he ran back to play.

"Oh, that's okay, Four-Eyes!" laughed Bee Bopp in a screeching sort of way. "I just love being bumped! Are those glasses on your face or are you modeling pop-bottle bottoms? Gee whiz, what a moth mouth!"

Glance just stood there with a buggball in his hands while the other kids joined Bee Bopp in her cruel laughter.

After recess Bee Bopp went to her class which was taught by Mizz Buggly. The new bugg wasted no time at all. She whispered just as loud as can be, "Gee whiz! What a dumb name. Buggly rhymes with ugly!"

The other buggs in class laughed and laughed, but then became very quiet as Mizz Buggly stormed down the aisle to where Bee Bopp was sitting. "What did you say?" she asked grimly.

"I said 'Buggly rhymes with ugly.' What's the matter, have you got a pencil stuck in your ear?" Bee Bopp giggled.

This time no one laughed. Mizz Buggly's face got just as red as could be. Just like that, before you could say "gee whiz" twice, Bee Bopp was on her way to the principal's office.

The principal sat behind his massive desk and looked at Bee Bopp sitting in a chair, popping her gum and looking around as if she didn't have a care in the world. "Bee Bopp, we will not tolerate that kind of talk at Buttonwood School!" the principal scolded. You will apologize to Mizz Buggly and to the entire class. Do you understand?"

Bee Bopp looked for a moment as if she wanted to cry, but instead of crying she began to giggle. "Well, gee whiz? Of course I understand, Mold Mouth. What do you think I am, dumb?"

The principal had never been spoken to so rudely, he picked up the phone and called Bee Bopp's parents. Within minutes, their bright red car screeched to a stop at Buttonwood School.

Mr. and Mrs. Mouth showed up just as Bee Bopp was telling the principal that he reminded her of a slithery worm in the Clover Forest. Farley T. just laughed and laughed, "Well, old pal principal, buggs will be buggs. Bee Bopp is such a card. She cracks me up!" But the principal wasn't laughing.

"Golly gee," said Melba Z., "we've had to move five times in the last four months, and wherever we go little Bee Bopp makes everybugg laugh and laugh." But still the principal wasn't laughing.

Finally he cleared his throat, "Ahem!" said he.

Bee Bopp couldn't resist. "Gee whiz, what's the matter? Have you got a frog in your throat or a toad on your tongue?" Her parents nearly rolled on the floor in laughter. This time the principal quietly wrote on a piece of paper and shoved it across the desk. It read, "Bee Bopp is hereby suspended from Buttonwood School!"

The Mouth family drove off laughing in the bright red car. "Well, little girl," her father laughed, "I guess we'll have to find you a private tutor or two."

"Golly gee," said Melba Z., "Lord and Lady Bugg live right next door. I'm sure they'd just love to tutor Bee Bopp!"

Then, in a puff of dust and leaves, they drove to old Bugg Manor, the home of Lord and Lady Bugg.

The old couple agreed to tutor Bee Bopp because they loved little bugg children. They took her into the parlor, and while Lord Bugg was getting some books and paper Bee Bopp started making jokes about Lady Bugg. "Gee whiz. Is that your nose or are you modeling buttons?" Bee Bopp roared with laughter, but Lady Bugg just sat on the settee and smiled a secret smile.

When Lord Bugg came back with the books Bee Bopp stuck out her foot and tripped him. The books went one way and he went the other. "Gee whiz!" she snickered. "What are you, some sort of fumble foot bugg?" Old Lord Bugg just lay on the floor and smiled a secret smile.

They tried to teach her the whole day long, but all she did was crack jokes and try to get them to laugh. The best she could do was to get the old bugg couple to smile their secret smiles.

Finally, just before she left to go home for the day, she turned all the pictures in the parlor upside down. "That will get them for sure." She skipped out the door and was racing down the cobbled walk when Lord Bugg called from inside the house, "Bee Bopp, could you come back here, please?"

Oh, joy! Finally she had their attention.

Thinking that they might be mad at her, Bee Bopp planned some funny things to say when she got in the house. But they weren't mad. Lord and Lady Bugg sat on the settee and sipped some tea and politely asked her to sit down.

She sat with a thump in a chair, and waited for them to start yelling.

"Be Bopp, we're not mad at you." said Lady Bugg in her quiet way.

"Why not?" Bee Bopp asked. For the first time in her life, she didn't know what to say.

"Because," said old Lord Bugg, "you don't really mean to hurt anybugg. You are just looking for attention. You've been moved from school to school, and the only way you can get anybugg to notice you is to be loud and funny. Sometimes Lady Bugg calls me funny names and tricks me to get my attention. Sometimes I laugh, sometimes I don't. But we understand because we are lonely, too!"

For the first time ever, Bee Bopp didn't laugh. Instead, she cried.

Bee Bopp and Lord and Lady Bugg soon became the best of friends. Sometimes they told jokes and sometimes they didn't. Sometimes they laughed and sometimes they cried. Late every afternoon they always drank tea and ate honeyed crumpets together, and they were never lonely again!

If you know someone noisy
as only a Bee Bopp can,
give them a little friendship
and try to understand.

BUGG
BOOKS™

PRINTED IN BELGIUM BY
proost
INTERNATIONAL BOOK PRODUCTION